THE NATIVITY
FOR CHILDREN

DIRECTLY FROM THE BIBLE

Scripture quotations are taken from the Holy Bible, New American Bible Revised Edition (Abbr. NABRE, Modern English, 2011, Copyright © Confraternity of Christian Doctrine).
Parts of the Bible's original text have been cut for simplicity.

Copyright © 2022 Kidsup Publishing. All rights reserved.

A Gift for:

....

From:

....

Contents

The angel Gabriel was sent from God to a town called Nazareth to Mary betrothed to a man named Joseph. And coming to her, he said, "Hail, favored one! The Lord is with you."

Then the angel said to her, "Do not be afraid, Mary, for you have found favor with God. You will bear a son, and you shall name him Jesus. He will be great and called Son of the Most High."

Part 1. The Annunciation

The Visitation - Luke 1:26-33

NAZARETH

5

But Mary said to the angel, "How can this be, since I have no husband?" And the angel said to her in reply, "The holy Spirit will come upon you, and the power of the Most High will overshadow you. Therefore the child to be born will be called holy, the Son of God. Mary said, "Behold, I am the handmaid of the Lord. May it be done to me according to your word." Then the angel departed from her.

Part 1. The Annunciation

Mary's Obedience to God - Luke 1:34-38

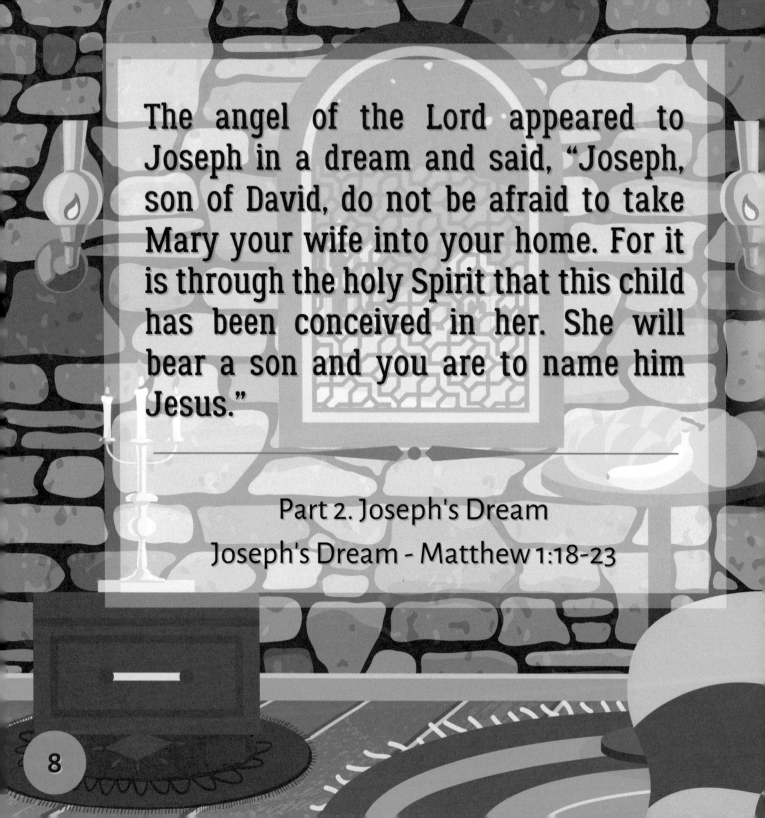

The angel of the Lord appeared to Joseph in a dream and said, "Joseph, son of David, do not be afraid to take Mary your wife into your home. For it is through the holy Spirit that this child has been conceived in her. She will bear a son and you are to name him Jesus."

Part 2. Joseph's Dream

Joseph's Dream - Matthew 1:18-23

When Joseph awoke, he did as the angel of the Lord had commanded him and took his wife into his home.

Part 2. Joseph's Dream

Joseph's Dream - Matthew 1:24

In those days a decree went out that the whole world should be enrolled. So all went to be enrolled, each to his own town. And Joseph too went up from the town of Nazareth to the city of David that is called Bethlehem, because he was of the house and family of David, to be enrolled with Mary, his betrothed, who was with child.

Part 3. Birth of Jesus and Shepherds Travel to Bethlehem - Luke 2:1-5

13

While they were there, the time came for her to have her child, and she gave birth to her firstborn son. She wrapped him in swaddling clothes and laid him in a manger, because there was no room for them in the inn.

Part 3. Birth of Jesus and Shepherds

Mary, Joseph, and Jesus - Luke 2:6-7

Now there were shepherds in that region living in the fields and keeping the night watch over their flock. The angel of the Lord appeared to them, and the glory of the Lord shone around them.

The angel said to them, "Do not be afraid; I proclaim to you good news of great joy. For today in the city of David a savior has been born for you who is Messiah and Lord. And this will be a sign for you: you will find an infant wrapped in swaddling clothes and lying in a manger."

Part 3. Birth of Jesus and Shepherds

The Angel and Shepherds - Luke 2:8-12

17

And suddenly there was a multitude of the heavenly host with the angel, praising God and saying:
"Glory to God in the highest and on earth peace to those on whom his favor rests."

Part 3. Birth of Jesus and Shepherds

The Multitude of the Angels - Luke 2:13-14

When the angels went away from them to heaven, the shepherds went in haste and found Mary and Joseph, and the infant lying in the manger. When they saw this, they made known the message that had been told them about this child. All who heard it were amazed. And Mary kept all these things in her heart.

Part 3. Birth of Jesus and Shepherds
The Visit of the Shepherds - Luke 2:15-20

BETHLEHEM

When Jesus was born in Bethlehem of Judea, in the days of King Herod, magi from the east arrived in Jerusalem, saying, "Where is the newborn king of the Jews? We saw his star at its rising and have come to do him homage."

When King Herod heard this, he was greatly troubled.

Then Herod sent the magi to Bethlehem and said, "Go and search diligently for the child. When you have found him, bring me word, that I too may go and do him homage."

Part 4. The Visit of the Magi

King Herod and the Magi - Matthew 2:1-8

After their audience with the king they set out. And behold, the star that they had seen at its rising preceded them, until it came and stopped over the place where the child was. And on entering the house they saw the child with Mary his mother. They prostrated themselves and did him homage. Then they opened their treasures and offered him gifts of gold, frankincense, and myrrh. And having been warned in a dream not to return to Herod, they departed for their country by another way.

BETHLEHEM

Part 4. The Visit of the Magi

The Visit of the Magi - Matthew 2:9-12

When they had departed, the angel of the Lord appeared to Joseph in a dream and said, "Rise, take the child and his mother, flee to Egypt, and stay there. Herod is going to search for the child."

Part 4. The Visit of the Magi
The Flight to Egypt - Matthew 2:13

EGYPT

BETHLEHEM

27

One night, 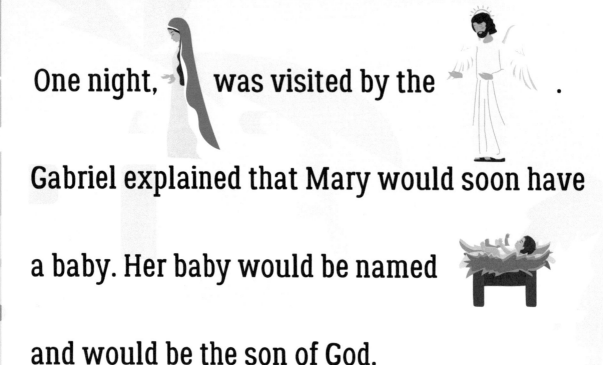 was visited by the .

Gabriel explained that Mary would soon have

a baby. Her baby would be named

and would be the son of God.

Mary   Angel   Jesus

Practice and consolidation of Bible knowledge

 and packed their bags and

traveled to Bethlehem to register for the census.

Mary was pregnant, so she was riding

on a  . When they came there, the only

place they could find to stay was a  .

 Joseph   Donkey   Stable

This was a magical night. 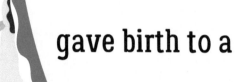 gave birth to a beautiful baby, . That night, there were  staying in the fields nearby, guarding their flocks of . The 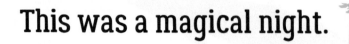 of God appeared to them, telling them good news.

Shepherds | Sheep | Jesus

 visited the newborn Savior and hurried to tell everyone about his birth. followed the  to  . They found in a manger and brought him gifts of gold, frankincense, and myrrh.

 Magi

 Star

 Bethlehem

So now you know the story of Christmas and how the Savior of the World started his journey on Earth. Many years after this day, Jesus is showing us how much he loves us. He came to the world to bring us love, joy, peace, and hope.

Thank you, God, for sending Jesus!

Merry Christmas

We'd be super grateful if you could spare a few minutes to leave us a review. Thank you for reading!

Made in United States
Troutdale, OR
12/12/2023

15809274R00021